E   J
782.42   c.1
JOE   1 COMPACT DISC
Joel
New York state of mind

Vermillion Public Library
18 Church Street
Vermillion, SD 57069
(605) 677-7060

DEMCO

NEW YORK STATE OF MIND

BY BILLY JOEL
ILLUSTRATED BY IZAK

Scholastic Press · New York

GEORGE WASHINGTON BRIDGE

Some folks like to get away
Take a holiday from the neighborhood

Hop a flight to Miami Beach or to Hollywood

HUDSON RIVER

But I'm taking a Greyhound on the Hudson River Line

I'm in a New York state of mind

TURN PERMITTED
6 AVE / PARK AVE / 3 AVE
10 AM - 6 PM

Music Hall RADIO CI

PRESENT THE RADIO CITY CHRISTMAS SPECTAC

Been high in the Rockies under the evergreens

ROCKEFELLER CENTER

I'm in a New York state of mind

BETHESDA FOUNTAIN

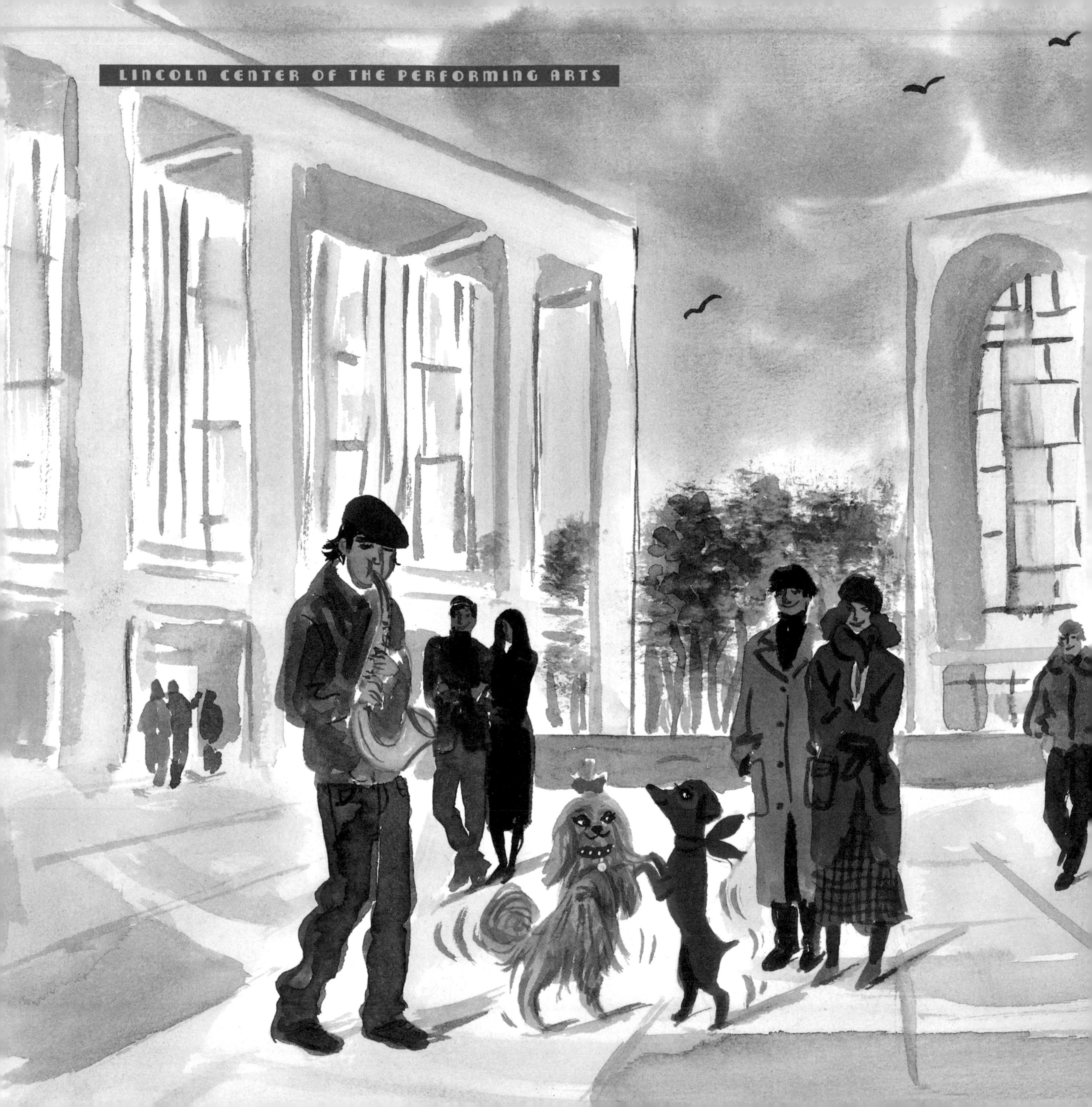
LINCOLN CENTER OF THE PERFORMING ARTS

It was so easy living day by day
Out of touch with the rhythm and blues

But now I need a little give and take
The *New York Times*, The *Daily News*

TROMP

It comes down to reality
And it's fine with me 'cause I've let it slide

I don't have any reasons
I've left them all behind

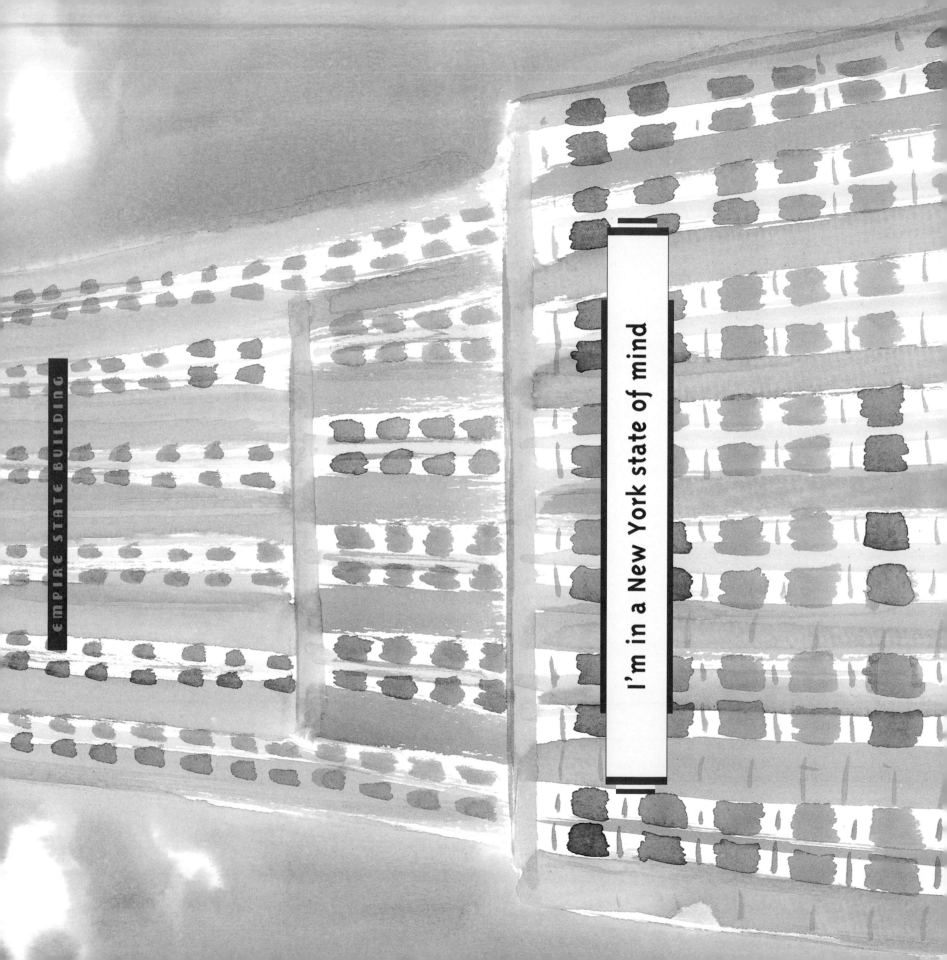

EMPIRE STATE BUILDING

I'm in a New York state of mind

This book is for everyone who lives in New York or who comes and falls in love with it.
No matter where you go in the world, you never really leave New York and it never really leaves you.
— B. J.

To my beloved daughter, Emmanuelle Aviva, and
to the magical city of New York that still fills my dreams.
— I. Z.

A Byron Preiss Book

Text copyright © 1976 Joelsongs (BMI)
Illustrations copyright © 2005 by Voyages, Inc. and Byron Preiss Visual Publications, Inc.
All rights reserved. Published by Scholastic Press, an imprint of Scholastic Inc., *Publishers since 1920*. SCHOLASTIC, SCHOLASTIC PRESS,
and associated logos are trademarks and/or registered trademarks of Scholastic Inc.

No part of this publication may be reproduced, stored in a retrieval system, or transmitted in any form
or by any means, electronic, mechanical, photocopying, recording, or otherwise, without written permission of the publisher.
For information regarding permission, write to Scholastic Inc., Attention: Permissions Department, 557 Broadway, New York, NY 10012.

Library of Congress Cataloging-in-Publication Data

Joel, Billy.
New York state of mind / by Billy Joel ; illustrated by Izak Zenou.— 1st ed.
p. cm.
"A Byron Preiss book."
Summary: Presents an illustrated version of performer Billy Joel's popular song celebrating New York City.
ISBN 0-439-55382-2 (alk. paper)
[1. New York (N.Y.) — Songs and music. 2. Songs.] I. Izak Zenou, ill. II. Title.

PZ8.3.J585Ne 2005   782.42164'0268 — dc22   2004020656

10 9 8 7 6 5 4 3 2 1   05 06 07 08 09

Book design by Elizabeth B. Parisi

Printed in Singapore 46 • First edition, November 2005